# Angela Anaconda ™

# Nannoying Nanette

POCKET
B O O K S

Based on the TV series *Angela Anaconda*®
created by Joanna Ferrone and Sue Rose as seen on Channel 4

First published in 2001 by Simon & Schuster Inc.
This revised edition first published in 2001 by Pocket Books with new illustrations
An imprint of Simon & Schuster UK Limited
Africa House, 64-78 Kingsway, London WC2B 6AH

Design & imaging by Threefold Ltd ©Simon & Schuster UK Ltd

ISBN 07434 15817

1 3 5 7 9 10 8 6 4 2

Printed in Hong Kong by Midas

# CONTENTS

STORY NUMBER ONE

# ice-BReakers

## Chapter 1

If you'd like to know what my name is, it is Angela Anaconda of the third grade, taught by Mrs Brinks. At my school, Tapwater Springs Elementary, I am mostly good, except for some of the time. And those times are practically always on account of a person in my class named Nanette Manoir, who pretends to be French but is not. She is the person who bugs me the most of anyone else. So you won't be surprised when I tell you about how she ruined my first-ever ice-skating lesson.

First of all, I just have to say I was really excited about learning how to ice-skate. And my dad is driving me and my friends Gina Lash and Johnny Abatti to our first-ever skating lesson any of us have ever had.

The roads are really slippery, but I am not one bit worried, because my dad invents cool inventions. And he invented one called the Ice Be-Gone, on account of it melts ice on contact whenever you pull the cord that's attached to the bottle that's attached to our car.

So we are on our way to pick up my other friend, Gordy Rhinehart, when the car wheels start spinning on the ice.

"Let 'er rip, Angelwings," my dad says. Angelwings is one of the names he calls me sometimes.

I quickly yank on the cord, and the car stops skidding, just like that!

"Ice Be-Gone does it again," says my dad, the coolest guy in the world.

Then we pull up in front of Gordy's house. He is standing there with Coach Rhinehart, his dad, waiting for us. Coach Rhinehart opens our car door. "Go get 'em, Gorderino!" he says, clapping Gordy on the back. This makes Gordy fall down, on account of Gordy is so very skinny and his dad is so very not.

But that's okay. Gordy just picks himself up and gets into our car, next to Gina Lash. "Don't break too many hearts," Gordy's dad says with a wink, and off we go.

"I brought you some Fishy Fish, Gina," says Gordy to Gina Lash, who he secretly loves. And he starts getting all wheezy like he always does when Gina's next to him.

Me and Gina and Johnny help ourselves because Fishy Fish Candies are our favourites! Except like now when they're hard as rocks on account of they got frozen when Gordy was waiting outside in the freezing cold. Everybody spits them out, even Gina Lash, who will normally eat just about anything.

When we pull up to the ice-skating pond we are so excited, we can hardly wait to put on our skates. But then something not so exciting happens ... You will see what I mean after I tell you who else's car is driving up to the rink ... Mrs Brinks!

"Mrs Brinks!" I'm the one who says, "What's she doing here? This isn't our school!"

"You don't think ..." Gordy wheezes ... "she's going to be ... our ice-skating teacher, do you?"

"No way, it's Saturday. Teachers can't teach on Saturdays," says Gina. "It's against union regulations – unless she's a scab."

Like I told you, Mrs Brinks is our most unfavourite teacher. And I don't think you'll be surprised that we are surprised to see her at our ice-skating pond. And we aren't very happy about it, either. But then her husband, Mr Brinks, whose name is Connie, gets out of their car. We hear her tell him, "Be sure you're waiting by the kerb at exactly one-fifteen!"

"Yes, dear," says Mr Brinks, his voice like a mouse.

The car door slams shut, and the car drives away, taking

Mrs Brinks away with it, which is lucky for us.

All of us say, "Phew. So it's Mr Brinks who's gonna be our teacher!"

"That's right, kids," says my dad. "Guess it's good he's dressed ... for the ice." And then he winks.

Mr Brinks's glasses sparkle in the sun. He wears strange-looking fuzzy red earmuffs and a long coat with furry stuff on the collar.

"I'm just glad he's wearing clothes at all," says Gina.

We all laugh at that one, even my dad. See, we all think Mr and Mrs Brinks are nudists who like to spend their weekends nude.

If this makes you think about the Brinkses ice-skating naked, then you're just like me. But I don't think about it for long. Yuck. Ugh. Gross.

## Chapter 2

So then we step out of the car and wave good-bye to my dad. Gordy Rhinehart takes off his coat. And he is wearing a shimmery, ruffly shirt, just like they wear on TV.

Johnny Abatti is dressed to play hockey, even though he doesn't know how to skate yet. Gina Lash looks puffier than she usually does in her puffy red parka. We put on our skates and step onto the ice verrry carefully.

Mr Brinks is taking forever to check off our names. Meanwhile all of us can barely stand up. My ankles keep caving in. Gina keeps falling down on her behind.

Mr Brinks has an official attendance list on his clipboard. "Okay, Angela is here, so I'll just put a little tick in this box

next to her name. And . . . Gina's here, tick. And Gordy's also here, so that's another little tick ..."

So far it is not so fun on account of it is not fun waiting for Mr Brinks to finish, and not fun trying to stand up on my skates. I am so busy trying to keep my ankles from caving in that I almost miss what Mr Brinks says next.

"Hmm, where's Nanette Manoir?"

This can't be, I think to myself – Nanette is going to ice-skate too? And then the next thing that happens is that I hear a voice. Her voice. Ninnie-Poo's voice.

"Over here! I'm over here!"

Am I just imagining things? No such luck. I look over and see it, the Manoirs' gigantic black giant-sized Town Car.

Nanette stands there, in a stupid plaid coat, shaking her golden, baloney curls. Their gardener, Alfredo, is bending down to shovel a path through the snow for her. What is she doing at our ice-skating class, is what I want to know, and besides, I thought the cold isn't good for her sensitive, un-French skin!

12

"I'm simply waiting for Alfredo to clear a path for me," she calls to us. "It's so hard keeping gardeners busy in the winter, and I certainly don't want to get any snow on my new *après*-skate boots!"

Then Alfredo helps her step out of her *après*-skate boots for snot-noses and into her skates.

"Wow, Nanette," says Gordy Rhinehart, staring at her boots. "Those boots are so next year."

"They're more than just next year, Gordy Rhinehart," says Nanette as she steps onto the ice. "They're pure ermine-lined *après*-skate boots!"

She twirls around on the ice, and it is at this point that it comes into my mind that she is not a beginner skater. She swooshes to a show-off stop near where we are standing, or at least trying to stand, covering all of us with a layer of ice.

"Well done, Nanette!" says Mr Brinks, clapping with his mittens. "Now let us begin. Please be very careful. We don't want any strains, sprains, or other nasty pains. Everyone follow me. Step, step, gliiiiiiide. Step, step, gliiiiiiide."

Me and Gordy and Johnny try to follow Mr Brinks. Gina

just falls on her butt. Ninnie-Poo flies past us. "Look at me! I can do it backwards!" she calls.

"Very nice, Nanette!" calls Mr Brinks. "But remember: A slow skater is a safe skater!"

"I don't want to go slow," Bratette says as she skates circles around us.

"Whatever you say, Nanette," Mr Brinks tells her.

Oh brother, I think.

"Hey!" yells Gina Lash. "Wasn't this supposed to be a beginners' class?" And then she falls down again.

"Yeah, Nanette!" I yell. "For someone who has never been in one before!"

"But you see," calls Ninnie-Poo, "I've never been in a public skating class, Angela Anaconda. I've only had private lessons, *à la carte!*"

"Come along, everybody," Mr Brinks is saying. "Heads up. Arms out. Step, step, gliiiiiiide."

"When are we gonna learn the slap shot?" asks Johnny Abatti.

Nanette just keeps showing off. She whooshes past Gina Lash and makes her fall onto her behind again.

"Step, step, gliiiiiiide," Mr Brinks keeps saying over and over again.

And then, if you can believe it, Gordy Rhinehart all of a sudden looks like he knows how to do it. "Hey, look! I'm gliding! I'm gliiiiiiiiding, everybody!" he calls, and his ruffles ruffle in the wind.

"Well, look at me!" cries Nanette as she zooms past. "I'm really skating!"

"Oh, my!" says Mr Brinks. "Aren't you the bee's naked knees! Impressive, Nanette, very impressive! Look, Angela. Look, Gina. See how she does it?"

Yeah, sure, more like, I see how she ruins our class. So, just like usual, Nanette Manoir is the teacher's pet. "We'd better learn to skate soon, Gina Lash," I tell my friend. "My ankles are tired!"

"Your ankles and my butt," says Gina, falling down again.

Nanette swoops up to Johnny Abatti. "Bonjour, John. Care to skate with a real skater?"

She grabs him by the hand. Which is something she always tries to do. Except that this time she starts to spin him around and around, faster and faster. There is no way he can stop or do anything except yell, "WHOAAA!"

Mr Brinks thinks it is great. "Magnificent! Wonderful!" he says. Then, all of a sudden, he must have stopped thinking it was so great. "Oh, my!"

Nanette has come to a sudden stop.

"Ta-da!" she says.

But Johnny Abatti does not come to a sudden stop. When Nanette lets go of his hand, he goes flying. And when he goes flying, you won't believe where he goes flying to.

"John!" I hear Ninky-Slinky say. "'Ta-da' means 'the end'! Come back here this instant!"

But Johnny Abatti cannot come back. He is too busy flying across the ice, without being able to stop, straight past Gordy and Gina, and crashes into me.

My life flashes before my eyes.

## Chapter 3

So, thanks to Ninnie-Poo Manoir and her unbeginner ice-skating, my broken arm gets broken. And I have to listen to my dumb brothers say dumb things. My brother Derek says, "Geez, Angie-pants, didn't they teach you how to fall?"

"Yeah," says my brother Mark, "maybe you need lessons on how to take skating lessons."

See what I mean? But the good thing is that I got a Day-Glo cast, and all of my friends at school want to sign it.

The bad thing is that Candy May is the first one in my class to try to sign it, and she takes forever to sign her name. She's just got to the 'a' in 'Candy', when who should open her big un-French mouth but Nanette.

"Excuse me, Mrs Brinks, but since it's taking Candy May such a long time to sign Angela Anaconda's cast, perhaps we need an example of proper signature form. And since I study calligraphy with the famous French calligrapher, Pierre La

Plume, I would be more than happy to volunteer."

And then Mrs Brinks, who thinks that Nanette Manoir is some kind of a genius, says, "Why, thank you, Nanette dear. How very generous of you to share your refined skills with the class."

And the next thing I know, Nanette has grabbed the pen out of Candy May's hand and is writing her name in huge big letters that take up my whole entire cast.

That night I sit on my bed and look down at my cast that she has wrecked. It doesn't do any good to turn the light off, because my Day-Glo cast glows in the dark so I can still see her name. I am stuck with it. Oh brother, I think, and then I turn the light on, then I turn it off, then on, then off.

And then in my mind I start thinking. I do a lot of making things up in my head, which my dad says is fine to do. In my head I can imagine anything I want, even if it's about things I would like to do to a Certain Nasty Someone that she actually deserves but that I wouldn't actually be allowed to do in real life. I would only imagine doing them. So this is what I imagine doing:

*Here comes Ninnie-Poo, Star of the Nanette Scapades, me the Skating Announcer Angela Anaconda announces! Watch as she and Gliding Gordy glide through their routine. The naked judges, who all happen to look just like Mr Brinks, say, don't you look divine, Ninky-Wink. The bee's naked knees, Little Nin.*

*The crowd is cheering on account of your excellent performance, but too bad Gordy Rhinehart only knows one move. I like to glide, he will tell you, as he picks you up and twirls you around, then throws you flying through the air.*

*Whoops! Watch out, Little Nin, I say as you land on your behind. That ice sure is slippery. Perhaps my dad's Ice Be-Gone is just what you need. Here comes Angela Anaconda to the rescue,*

*I will tell you while I spray the Ice Be-Gone all around you. Oops. So sorry, Little Nin, but it appears you have fallen right through the hole I have accidentally made in the ice.*

*"Save me! Save me!" you will tell me as you splash around in the icy water wearing nothing but your fancy pink skating outfit. "These waters are filled with millions of Fishy Fish who would like to chew on my sensitive skin!"*

*Bye-bye, Nanook of the North, I will tell you as you float out to sea and the Land of the Midnight Sun, which is what I think they call Alaska. Here come the Eskimo babies, who learned to skate before they could even walk. Uh-oh! They have built an igloo out of you! Or should I say ... UG-loo!*

*But here comes Angela, paddling up in my kayak. Never fear, my fake French friend, I will gladly come to your rescue, except – look! You are frozen just like a hockey puck! In fact, here comes Johnny Abatti, who really thinks you are a hockey puck, my prissy polar pal.*

*"Help me, help me, Oh Great One, Angela Anaconda, whose skating ability would be far superior to mine if I, Nanette, hadn't so rudely interrupted your beginners' class and broken*

21

*your arm," you will tell me.*

*But then when I come to rescue you, I can't help thinking, did somebody say, Na-NET?*

*Then, WHAM! Into the net Hockey Puck Nanette will go! Angela ONE, Nincompoop . . . NOTHING! The crowd goes wild and they all yell, "An-ge-la! An-ge-la! An-ge-la!"*

"An-ge-la! ANGELA!"

Oops. I open my eyes and I am no longer imagining things. It is morning! My friends Gina, Gordy and Johnny are standing outside my bedroom window, calling my name – "An-ge-la!" The sun is streaming in.

"Hey, Angela! We're going to shovel snow for the shut-ins!" calls Gina Lash. "Want to come?"

"You bet," I yell down to them.

## Chapter 4

So there I am with my friends, blasting away the snow with my bottle of Ice Be-Gone because, on account of my broken arm, I can't shovel like Gina, Johnny and Gordy. Then all of a sudden we hear a rumble from across the street.

And going towards the Manoirs' driveway is Alfredo, driving a tractor, and attached to the tractor is a fancy little sledge and on the sledge is none other than Nanette Manoir and her poofy French poodle, Oo-la-la, getting a free ride as usual. The tractor stops right in front of us, spraying snow all over where we have just cleared it.

"Oh, I am ever so sorry," says Nanette, who does not sound one bit sorry at all. "I'd gladly offer to help if I weren't wearing my pure ermine-lined *après*-skate boots, which would be ruined if just a speck of snow were to touch them. So if you'll excuse me, I'll just go drink some *imported* hot chocolate in front of our *roaring* fireplace! *Bonne chance!*"

We watch them drive away, this time spraying even more snow where we have been clearing it. Across the street, which is where the Manoirs live, we watch Ninnie-Poo step out of her boots and hand them to Alfredo. Then she goes inside.

Then we see Alfredo give us a look. He puts the boots down, right there on the driveway. And he looks at us again.

That is when we get an idea.

"Are you thinking what I'm thinking, Angela Anaconda?" says Gina Lash.

"If you're thinking what I'm thinking," I tell her.

And then three shovels full of snow belonging to Gina, Johnny and Gordy just happen to land on those pure ermine-lined *après*-skate boots by accident. Accidentally on purpose!

We all stare at the boots with the lumps of snow in them. And then we hear the tractor again. And along comes Alfredo on the tractor. He revs the engine and winks at us, and then does something we never expected him to do. He dumps a huge pile of snow on top of Nanette's fancy boots.

By the time we have already almost fallen down in the snow from laughing, I say, "Good thing those boots are so next year, Gordy Rhinehart. Because I don't think Ninnie-Poo's going to be seeing them until next spring!"

STORY NUMBER TWO
# Fairweather Friends

## Chapter 1

$O$ne day at school, we were all set to be bored by Mrs Brinks when we got a big surprise.

"Class," said Mrs Brinks as if she was about to cry. "Nanette Manoir will not be gracing our classroom with her radiant presence today. I'm afraid she's home sick in bed with a head cold and laryngitis."

"Say it isn't so!" cried January.

"Say it isn't so even more!" cried Karlene.

"Yippee!" I wanted to cry.

This day is going to be even

better than even I thought. Then Mrs Brinks told us we had to each write a nice get well note to poor sick Nanette. I don't know if it was because I was wearing my all-purpose jungle pith helmet (which January and Karlene always made fun of) or not, but suddenly I had a great idea: "Nanette, I know you're sick. I'm just sorry you're ill", I wrote. Now everybody (except Mrs Brinks and Ninnie Wart's suck up friends) know that Nanette is sick in the head at least, so that part of my note was true. The "I'm just sorry you're ill" part of my note was not true, but hey, I was just trying to be polite. And good thing I was, because Mrs Brinks read my note and did not mind the first part of it at all. (I don't think she understood it.)

"Why Angela, that's very sweet," she said, a little surprised I had written something nice. (Again, I don't think she understood it and secretly what I wrote was not meant to be nice at all.)

Then she went on to explain that Nanette was "in charge" of the "Spring Fling" decorating committee, but since she was so sick, we had to pick someone else to fill her shoes. That's when Candy May raised her hand.

"What should we fill her shoes with?," she asked.

Now Candy May is not the smartest person in our class, but she does manage to do one thing right: she always confuses Mrs Brinks.

"I don't follow," said Mrs Brinks, looking confused.

"Follow who?" asked Candy May. If she tried, Candy May could not drive Mrs Brinks any crazier. Mrs Brinks just ignored Candy May's last question and then she held up a hat that she said had all our names in it. She said she was going to pick someone else to replace Nanette, her sick (in the head) pet, to be in charge of the Spring Fling decorations! Too bad Ninnie Wart was sick with laryngitis, otherwise she would be screaming right now in her un-French French.

"I will now choose a student at random who will take the place of poor Nanette. That student will be in charge of the Spring Fling decorations and shall choose two helpers to help decorate," said Mrs Brinks.

I was so happy that someone

31

else, not Nanothing Manoir, was going to be in charge, that I could not have even have dreamed of what was going to happen next.

"Why, it's Angela Anaconda!" said Mrs Brinks, pulling my name out of the hat. And because she thought I had also written a nice get well note to Nanette (which she didn't understand was really just a joke), she was actually glad she picked my name!

"Hey everybody! I'm in charge!" I was yelling on account of I was so happy. I had never been put in charge of anything except cleaning erasers in Mrs Brinks's class. I did not even think about how mad Nanette would be when she read my "nice" get well note, which was not very nice at all.

**I**n the lunchroom later that day, all of a sudden being in charge made me very important. I was sitting with Gina Lash, Johnny Abatti and Gordy Reinhart eating my lunch and minding my own business, when suddenly everybody wanted me to pick them as my helpers. And I mean everybody, especially those two no-bodies who want to be somebodies, named January and Karlene.

"Angela! Did I tell you I love your hat?" asked January.

"And I love it even more!" said Karlene.

"It's a pith helmet," I corrected. "It's what jungle explorers wear to keep pesky parasites out of their hair!" Both of them started laughing. That's how much they wanted to get on my good side. I wanted to remind them that this was the pith helmet that they always made fun of! But then Karlene's beeper started ringing and instead of answering it

33

she turned it off.

"Who cares, it's just Nanette," she said.

"Who wants to talk to her when we can talk to you?" said January.

"About what?" I asked.

"Oh, about why you should pick us as your Spring Fling helpers!" said Karlene.

As if I would ever pick *them* to help *me!* For one thing I had my three best friends, Gina Lash, Johnny Abatti and Gordy Reinhart sitting right next to me. In fact, I was just starting to wonder how I was going to pick only two of my three very best friends when January hands me some delicious Mallow Muffs to eat.

Then Karlene says: "And here's a whole squirt bottle of whipped cream, with your name on it!"

"Thanks," I said, as I squirted some into my

34

mouth. If being in charge made mean people be nice to you, I was not going to be the one to complain about it.

"Angela Anaconda, this is bribery," said Gina Lash. "They're only doing this so you'll pick them." Since Gina Lash is the smartest in the class, I had to agree with her. I gave the whipped cream back to Karlene (after Gina took some).

"Sorry, not interested," I said.

"Perhaps you would like to come swimming in my own private backyard swimming pool?" asked January.

"A real water-filled swimming pool built for swimming? Not a plastic blow-up baby ankle-wetter?" I asked.

"Angela, the legal term for this is extortion," said Gina Lash. Her, Johnny and Gordy were starting to get annoyed at me for even talking to these two no-bodies.

"You can invite your friends," said January, noticing how mad they were getting.

"And we'll have an all-you-can-eat barbecue!" said Karlene.

Suddenly Gina Lash didn't mind if it was bribery and extortion or not.

"Let me get this straight," Gina said. "We get to swim in a real pool and eat barbecue till we burst and those two can-kissers have to do all the decorating? I don't see the down side."

Johnny and Gordy didn't see any downside either.

So it was time for me to make a final decision.

"Attention, everyone," I yelled, standing on the table. "I need to make an announcement. I choose January Cole and Karlene Trainor as my official Spring Fling helpers!"

Well, you can't please all of the people all of the time. Most of the kids were disappointed, but not Gina, Gordy and Johnny because we were all getting a free barbecue and swimming party. And January and Karlene were hugging each other and jumping up and down as if they had just won the Miss America Beauty Contest.

## Chapter 3

That afternoon we all went to January's house to go swimming in her real water-filled swimming pool. Now, it must have been my pith helmet making me smarter again because I definitely came up with the best theme ever for our Spring Fling. Bugs and Worms! Of course January and Karlene did not get it. They wanted to do a flower theme which was not only predictable but exactly what Nanette Manoir would have done, which is why I thought of Bugs and Worms.

"Bugs and worms unfreeze in the spring and crawl and fly," I was telling them as I thought it out. "That's how you know its spring. The first mosquito bite!"

Even though they really thought it was disgusting, they had to make themselves agree with me that this was the best theme ever, because I was in charge and the in-charge person is always right. Since they would be doing all the work decorating the gym, I had plenty of time to think of what orders to give them. For the first time I understood what Ninnie Wart sees in these two dim Nin slaves of hers: they always agree and will do anything the person in charge tells them to. They even started wearing pith helmets like mine.

"This is the life," I said to Gina as I floated around January's pool two days later. The Spring Fling was only one day away. Gordy was still trying to get into his wet suit so he wouldn't get wet when he went into the water. Gina and Johnny were waiting for the delicious barbecue that Karlene was cooking, and January had put up a big sign that said: 'ANGELA ANACONDA – THE BEST, BETTER, BEST-EST LEADER PERSON IN CHARGE!' This certainly was the life and who could disagree with me? Gina Lash, that's who.

"It won't last," she said.

"Why shouldn't it last?" I asked. "January and Karlene think I'm funny and brilliant."

"And in charge," said

Gina. Then she looked across the lawn over towards Mrs Brinks's sick pet rat Nanette Manoir's house. I thought of how high Nanette's fever would get if she saw her little Copycat-Clone-Club now.

While I was bouncing around on the diving board, Johnny Abatti asked me: "Don't the decorations for the Spring Fling have to be done by tomorrow, Angela?"

It was true, we had been having so much fun at January's pool for the past two days, being waited on by Karlene, I hadn't done much about actually making the decorations. But I had come up with a very smart idea to make sure that the decorations got done.

"As the person in charge, I figured out a way to swim and dive and bounce and get the gym decorated: I put Candy May in charge!" I confessed in mid-air as I jumped into the pool.

SPLASH!

"Who's in charge?" Both clone drones demanded.

"Candy May," I said as I executed a perfect landing on my float.

"Pool party's over!" said Karlene as she pulled me out of

the pool, float and all. Then January pulled a switch and an electric cover rolled out and covered the pool.

"What's going on around here?" I asked. "How come all of a sudden I'm not so great?"

"We were only being nice to you because you were in charge," said January.

Karlene dialled her cell phone. "Hello, is Candy May there? Its an emergency of emergency proportions!"

Then January and Karlene took off, leaving us high and dry without either water or barbecue food.

"Hey!" I yelled after them. "Come back here before I take you off the decorating committee that I am no longer in charge of!"

Finally Gordy came outside dressed in his wet suit. He took one look at the covered-up pool and said: "Hey, I never even got to not get wet!"

"Yeah, and what about our barbecue?" asked Gina Lash.

Well, at that moment you could've cooked a barbecue on my head, I was so steaming mad!

# CHapTer 4

$A$s I stared into the sealed-up swimming pool I thought about how sorry January and Karlene would be, when I, Angela Anaconda, would become the world's fanciest fancy swimmer. Then I thought about how happy January and Karlene, my not-so loyal Spring Fling-ettes, would be to have a new leader to lead them. In my imagination, instead of January's plain old swimming pool, we would swim in a giant pool with fountains. And since they were my humble assistants, they would have to wear pith helmets the whole time.

*"Watch out, fickle flunkies," I will tell them as I swan dive into the pool, accidentally knocking them in. Since I am such a fancy swimmer, my fancy kicking would create a whirlpool which would instantly suck them under.*

*"And if you ever really think I'll ever be your real friend,*

definitely don't bother to hold your breath, pointless pop-up pals," I will warn them.

"Angela! Angela! Help us!" they will cry as they bob to the surface. "Oh great Spring Fling leader, better than Nanette!" But it is too late because I am already up on the high diving board.

"Sorry I can't hear you," I will call down to them. "On account of I am about to do my famous back-stabber cannon ball, with a double axle to grind." And then I will yell, "BOMBS AWAY," as I hit the water with such a giant splash that January and Karlene are thrown out of the pool and onto the pool deck where they land. Even though they are half drowned and spitting out water, they will still be clapping for me like trained seals.

"Thank you, my slimy slaves! Now catch this and our fair-weathered friendship will be SEALED,"

44

*I will tell them. As I throw them a beach ball, they throw it back and forth between their two snooty noses. And then I will feed my little pets all of the uncooked barbeque fish that Gina Lash never got to eat. And they will be up to their necks in raw fish in no time!*

In my mind, I can even hear the jealous squawks of pelicans, but then I realize it is not the pelicans who are rudely interrupting my daydream, but the baloney-headed boss of those two backstabbers herself ...

## Chapter 5

"Excusez-moi, Angela Anaconda, but just what do you think you're doing here?" screams Nanette Manoir as she is wheeled up to us in a wheelchair by her butler, Alfredo. Because she is so sick and weak she is speaking through a megaphone.

"January and Karlene invited us over for a swim," I tell her.

"Oh, please," she says as she gets out of her wheelchair and rips down the banner saying "ANGELA IS THE BESTEST LEADER".

"January and Karlene are spineless, but at least they have taste. You are going to be in so much trouble when they see what you've done to this yard, Angela Anaconda!" Then she stops and

looks around. "Hmm, where are January and Karlene?"

Suddenly the Nin Twins come skipping into the backyard following Candy May and wearing Candy May hairdos. And because Candy May is in charge, they are treating her as if she is the most brilliant person on earth (which she is not).

"We think filling the gymnasium from floor to ceiling with crunched up napkins to make a 'Freak Spring Snowstorm' is a brilliant idea, Candy May!" January says. Or is it Karlene?

"Nanette!" cried January, noticing her for the first time.

"You're not sick any more!" said Karlene.

"No, but from the looks of it, YOU two are!" said Nanette. "Alfredo, push me home! Hurry, before I catch whatever they have!"

January and Karlene ran after her, begging for her baloney-headed forgiveness.

Even a smart person would be confused by all this. So Candy May was even doubly confused.

"Am I still in charge of the party?" she asked me.

"Sorry, Candy May," I told her. "That party's over. But if

you want, you can be in charge of this one."

"You're having a party?" she asked. "I thought you said it was over."

"It's not over till the food's over," said Gina Lash, walking off towards January's kitchen.

And that's the one one thing about my friends: they may not care about who is in charge, but they sure know how to have fun.

# THE HOE-DOWN SHOW-DOWN

## CHAPTER 1

**M**y dad Bill is the most perfect dad in the world. He's a salesman, and he's also an inventor and one day he'll combine his two jobs and sell one of his inventions. Until then, I'm happy just having him around, inventing cool stuff that helps around the house.

But I have to tell you that today my dad is not so perfect, on account of he has entered us in a square-dancing contest, for square dancers.

When my Dad pulls the car into the Spangly Jangles parking lot and tells me to, "Giddy up, partner," I sink further down into my seat, hoping that no one sees me.

Once we're in the store, we start trying on Western shirts or "duds", as Dad calls them, which is what I really think they are: duds. And the worst part is that there are matching duds, as in we're both wearing the same ugly plaid shirt!

Right in the middle of our western wear modelling session, Spangly Jangles himself comes over. "Yee-haw! Blamed if it ain't ol' cowboy Bill himself!"

Dad and Spangly shake hands, on account of they're friends, because Dad sold Spangly a mechanical bull last year.

"How's she doing?" Dad asks, pointing to the electric bucking bronco across the room.

"She's still a-buckin' like a pony in a poppycock coop," says Spangly, "and the best part is I don't ever have to feed her."

Then Spangly does one of the coolest things I've ever seen. He spits a gigantic spit right through a big gap in his front teeth. It flies across the room and lands in a silver spittoon with a DING! I'm beginning to think that maybe this Spangly is a real cowboy, on account of who else but a real cowboy would spit like that?

"Well, sir, I kin see y'all have mighty fine taste in western duds, yessir," says Spangly, patting Dad on the shoulder. Then he turns to me. "And I got just the thang fer you, little buckaroo."

Spangly ducks into a back room and comes back with a pair of shiny metal spurs. He puts them on my heels and I take them for a test spin. *CHING, CHING, CHING!* My spurs actually "ching" every time I take a step. Maybe this hoe-down idea is not such a bad idea after all!

"Now you'll be square dancing with the best of 'em," says Spangly.

"Oh, you'll be square dancing with the best, all right, Angela Anaconda," says a voice from behind me. I turn around and see that the voice is coming from exactly who I was hoping it wasn't coming from – my most-hated enemy who I hate the most, Nanette Manoir!

## Chapter 2

**J**ust when something that wasn't supposed to be fun was starting to be fun, Ninnie-Poo shows up! And what makes matters worse is she's with her father, who thinks he is a real cowboy.

"Howdy you all," he says. Anyone knows a real cowboy would say 'y'all' instead of "you all", which proves he's about as much a cowboy as Nanette Manoir is French, which is not at all.

"We're here to purchase a whole 'passel', as they say, of western wear to donate to the less fortunate participants in this year's hoe-down," says Nanette's father, grabbing an armload of studded shirts marked eighty per cent off.

"You aren't actually going to wear that *faux* turquoise tie are you, ol' chap?" asks Mr Manoir, tugging on Dad's new tie.

Dad takes back his tie and changes the subject by asking Mr Manoir about his business.

"Business is booming as usual," says Mr Manoir. Then the mechanical bull across the room must have caught his eye, because Mr Manoir mentions the bull my father sold him six months ago.

Mr Manoir says he can't remember paying it off and asks Dad to send him a bill for whatever he owes and a receipt. "I'm donating the bull to the hoe-down. I need the receipt for the tax write-off, you understand."

I hope my dad understands, because I sure don't.

"Of course, the real big hit of the hoe-down will be my Cactus Flower and me do-si-do-ing our way to yet another square dance victory," says Mr Manoir, patting his cactus flower – otherwise known as Ninnie-Pinhead Manoir – on the head.

"What will that make it, Daddy?" asks Nanette. "Two years in a row?"

Two years in a row that you have been an annoying un-French loser, I think.

Mr Manoir smiles smugly. "Actually, Cactus, after we win this year, we'll have three victories under our cowboy belts."

"I wouldn't be clearing a space for that trophy just yet,"

says Dad, saving the day like he usually does. "Angela and I are entering the competition this year, and we might just give you a run for your money."

Nanette turns to her dad, all full of fake smiles. "Daddy," she coos, "if the Anacondas are going to be in this year's hoe-down, shouldn't we buy Angela a proper western outfit? After all, we *are* donating western wear to the less fortunate participants."

Nanette points to my socks, which are sagging. "And look, Angela Anaconda's socks are so old they keep falling down into her boots!"

I'm about to tell Nanette that the reason my socks keep falling is because they want to get as far away from her ugly face as much as I do, when Dad steps in.

"I'm sure Nanette knows her offer is entirely unnecessary," Dad says.

"C'mon Bill," says Howell. "It's not like your daughter couldn't use some sprucing up. After all, she's not going to get noticed for her dancing."

Suddenly Dad's eyes narrow and his face

gets red. "That does it, Howell!" he yells. "You can insult my business, you can even insult my tie, but nobody insults my daughter's do-si-do! Nobody! I challenge you to a hoe-down show-down."

Mr Manoir and my dad stare at each other for a long time. If it *really* was the Old West and they really were cowboys, I bet they'd have their hands on their holsters. Then Mr Manoir reaches into his pocket, and for a second I think that maybe he does have a holster, but instead he just pulls out a big wad of cash.

"Why don't we make it a little more interesting, shall we?" Nanette's dad says, waving dollars in our face. "Say if we win, I won't have to pay you the money I owe on that mechanical bull you sold me."

"Okay," says Dad, "but if we win, you'll have to buy ten more bulls from me! Deal?"

"Deal!" answers Mr Manoir.

"And may the squarest dancer win."

## CHAPTER 3

So now it is up to my dad and me to practise like we've never practised before, which is a lot, on account of we haven't ever practised before. We have to learn how to square dance in time for the hoe-down show-down.

Luckily Dad has bought a practice tape with a practice announcer calling square-dancing steps for us to practise to. Only now I realize that not only do we have to dance along to what the announcer says, we have to dance along in rhyming dance steps. Whoever thought up square dancing must have thought about it a little too hard, because that's what it is – too hard!

"Swing your partner, do-si-do. Allemande left, to and fro," calls the announcer in a country twang. Dad and I try to do these things, except that when I go "to", he goes "fro", and we end up on the floor.

"Skip-to-my-Lou, don't step on her toes. Promenade, and 'round she goes." But step on my toes is exactly what he does.

"Sashay left an' sashay right. Swing your partner with all yer might," says the announcer. And Dad and I are starting to get it right! But just as he is about to swing me around, my socks fall down and I have to stop do-si-do-ing and pull them up.

"Hold it right there, Angel-fish," says Dad. "I have just the thing to make those saggy socks a thing of the past." Then he pulls a pair of cowboy boots out of a bag.

"Cowboy boots?" I ask.

"Not just any cowboy boots," says Dad. "Cowboy boots with my patented sock-lock system. They have super-sticky double-sided tape inside to stick to your socks, so they won't sag ever again."

I pull on the boots and the best part is, they actually work like they're supposed to work. Dad has done it again!

"Those Manoirs don't stand a chance," says Dad, and I am beginning to think that he is right.

## Chapter 4

Dad and I are dressed in matching western shirts that match, and I am wearing my sock-lock boots. We are ready as ready can be for the hoe-down show-down.

We get to the hoe-down extra early to pick out an extra-good dancing spot, but we aren't the only ones who are early. Nanette Manoir and her dad are already there warming up. And, can you believe it – they've brought along a dancing coach!

"Hello, Angela Anaconda. I'd like you to meet Pierre, our world-renowned choreographer who Daddy hired to help us perfect our already near perfect square-dancing moves," says Nanette, as she shows off her do-si-do's.

And then I hear a huge "YEE-HAW!" from across the room and turn and

64

see Spangly Jangles himself!

"Spangly!" I say. "Did you come to watch us dance the square dance?"

"Mr Jangles is one of the judges of tonight's contest," explains Nanette's dad, as he slips Spangly a big fat cheque with lots of big fat zeros. "Here," he says, "for all those duds I bought from you for the less fortunate."

"Woo-wee," says Spangly, pocketing the cheque, "you've just kept me in business for the next ten years!"

But so what if Spangly Jangles votes for the Man-worms on account of they bought a lot of duds. Dad says it is the square dance caller who can make you or break you. And if I were Ninnie-Poo, I would prepare to be broken!

Just then the square dance caller steps up to the microphone, and it's the same Pierre that had coached the Man-cheaters all of last week! "Didn't I tell you?" says Nanette. "Daddy is also donating the square dance caller."

And before I can yell that that is unfair, Pierre starts calling, so we

65

have to start dancing.

"It's contest time, so if you dare, grab your partners and form a square," says Pierre. "Allemande left and do a twist, do-si-do around like this. All join hands, raise up to the middle, hands out front like cakes on the griddle."

Dad and I start dancing, and we are actually not bad. We are Allemande-ing, do-si-do-ing, and hand-joining better than just about anyone, and definitely better than Nanette and her un-cowboy father. And Nanette knows it, because the next thing she does is wink at Pierre.

"Mix it up, Pierre," she says, and Pierre actually winks back, which is how I know that Dad and I are about to be in trouble.

"Switch your partner! Don't be shy! Time to dance with the other gal's guy!" Pierre calls.

Nanette grabs my dad and Nanette's dad grabs me and

before we know it, they are spinning us around and around until I am more dizzy than I've ever been in my short life.

"Now that you have got the knack, find your partner, switch them back," calls Pierre. Dad and I somehow stumble back to each other and immediately fall down on the ground. And the worst part is, while my dad and I are still trying to get up, Nanette and her dad are winning the contest right out from under us! Nanette grabs the trophy from the judges.

"My, my, my," says Howell. "It's even bigger than last year's – and the year before that!"

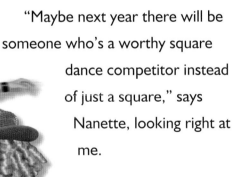

"Maybe next year there will be someone who's a worthy square dance competitor instead of just a square," says Nanette, looking right at me.

Suddenly my brain can't take it any more and I am about to explode. "Think of something to make yourself feel better," I think to myself. So, this is what I think:

Next time there is a square dance competition, I will call the moves. And when I am a square dance caller, Nanette will not be winning, I can promise you that, on account of she will have to do everything exactly as I tell her.

*Are you ready, Little Nin? Because my square dance will go a little something like this:*

*"Swing your partner, stub your toes, put your fingers up your nose."*

*Ninnie will clutch her painful foot in pain, but now is no time to stop dancing, on account of I am only getting started.*

*"Skip to my Lou, right down in the dumps. Look out! You're dancing in cow-pie clumps."*

69

*How does that smell, Nanette Manure? Sure doesn't smell like you'll win this show-down.*

*"Do-si-do with the mechanical bull, you'll never come off with sticky-tapes pull!"*

*That's right, Ninnie-loser, you'll finish this dance on the bucking bronco! But it will buck you right out the door as I finish my square dance calling:*

*The winner of this hoe-down is my dad and me. But you'll be too far away to see! The mechanical bull bucks you away, and I'll take my trophy because I won today!*

Suddenly I hear Nanette yelling, "Don't touch, it! You'll smudge the shine," and I realize that I'm accidentally holding the trophy.

"That's as close as you're ever going to get to winning a trophy, Angela Anaconda," declares Ninnie, yanking the trophy away from me.

"And that's as close as you'll ever be to getting paid for that mechanical bull," adds Mr Manoir, laughing at my dad.

But Dad smiles and I am thinking that maybe he has an idea. He turns to Spangly and says, "Hey, Spangly, don't you think the crowd should give the winners a big ol' western 'hat's off'?"

Dad takes his hat off and begins waving it at the Manoirs, as if he's actually glad they won. I can't believe my eyes!

"Dad, what are you doing?" I whisper.

"Trust me, Angel-fish," he says, still waving his hat. Then Spangly grabs the microphone from Pierre.

"Hey, folks," he says, "whadda y'all say we give a big ol' western cheer for the winners?" Spangly takes off his cowboy hat and waves it in the air yelling, "Yee-Haw," and everyone does the same thing.

The Manoirs look at each other and realize that the only polite thing to do is wave back. And we all know how polite they have to be. So they try to take off their hats, but for

71

some reason, the hats won't come off!

I look over at Dad and he is actually snickering.

"I had some super-sticky double-sided tape left over from those boots I fixed for you and I didn't want it to go to waste, so . . ."

"Yee-OUCH!" yells Nanette. "My hair! My hair!" Ninnie's hat is stuck to her bologna hair and she can't get it off. And then, Mr Manoir tugs at his hat with all his might and suddenly his toupee wig pulls right off of his head and he's standing there bald!

"See, Angel-wings?" says Dad, as he winks my way.

"I told you the hoe-down show-down would be fun."

# Fishing for Trouble

## Chapter 1

The only good thing about school is the school bell – well, that and lunch. And recess. And days when I get to run the slide projector and Nanette Manoir does not.

But right now, all I care about is waiting for the bell, on account of as soon as it rings, it's Friday afternoon and Friday afternoon means tomorrow is Saturday morning, and on Saturday morning I get to go fishing with my dad.

When the bell finally rings, I hurry home from school and find my mum in the kitchen, making lunches for us to take on our trip. That's when I ask to help out, on account of right now the only person with her is my baby sister Lulu, and I really don't think she's much help.

Mum and I have the sandwich-making going perfectly perfect (she's in charge of meat and cheese and I'm in charge of mustard and mayonnaise), when my stupid brothers, Mark and Derek, come in and ruin it.

Did I tell you that Mark and Derek are coming with us tomorrow? Probably not, on account of that's a fact I would like to forget. Mark reaches for a sandwich and I slap his hand. "Those are for tomorrow," I tell him.

Then Mark tries to grab another sandwich, but Derek grabs it first.

"Hey!" says Mark, looking like he's going to sock Derek in the face, and I hope he does, because then they'll get grounded and they won't be able to go fishing tomorrow. "You ate that whole sandwich in one bite! You rock!"

That's when I leave the kitchen because I can't

think about anything that I care about less than how Mark and Derek eat like pigs.

I walk into the garage and find my dad, who is hunched over, working on something. When he looks up, I see that he has his heavy-duty welding mask on.

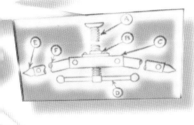

"Hi, Angel-fish," he says. "You'll never guess what invention I'm working on for tomorrow's fishing trip!"

## Chapter 2

Dad shows me the coolest thing I've seen since he showed me his last cool invention. "Behold the Whirl-a-Reel!" says Dad, holding it up.

I take a good look at the Whirl-a-Reel. It looks like a regular fishing rod, only the bottom of it is full of gears and buttons – even more than a regular fishing rod is full of gears and buttons. I reach out to take it, but Dad yanks it away.

"Don't touch it! It's still molten," Dad warns. "Besides, before you learn to use the Whirl-a-Reel, you've got to learn to fish! We'll just let this thing cool off."

Dad sets the Whirl-a-Reel on a shelf, grabs two fishing

rods from the corner and walks out into the front yard.

"You know what they say," says Dad. "Give a man a fish and he'll eat for a day. Teach a man to fish and he'll eat for a lifetime. Now here's how you cast."

Dad swings back his rod and lets the fishing line fly. It sails up, floating down gracefully and landing clear across the lawn.

"You try," says Dad, handing me the rod. I take the rod, swing it back, and let go – and the fishing line immediately gets caught in the bushes behind me.

"Takes practice," says Dad.

So we practise, and practise and practise, and by the time Mum calls us to dinner, I am casting so well that I've caught six flowers, two clumps of grass and an entire mailbox.

During dinner, Dad says I'll soon be ready to be introduced to the Whirl-a-Reel. "Your old man has almost finished the most amazing invention since the pocket fisherman. It reels in even the feistiest fishes with one tap of a button."

"If you can catch fish just by tapping a button, how come I just spent three hours learning how to cast a rod and wearing out my arm?" I ask.

"That's life, Angel-fish," replies Dad. I ask him if I can stay up and help him perfect the Whirl-a-Reel, but Dad says that I should get some sleep on account of tomorrow morning's going to be an early one.

## Chapter 3

I'm in the middle of dreaming that I'm a world-famous fisherman, when my dad wakes me up. I hop out of bed already ready to go, on account of I put on my rubber wading trousers the night before.

"Is it time for fishing?" I ask, but then Dad holds up his hands to show me that they're both all bandaged up in big white bandages!

"Uh, there's been a slight change of plan," explains Dad. "My Whirl-a-Reel was a little feisty. When I finished tweaking it, I took it for a test spin. The Whirl-a-Reel caught a tyre and reeled it right back into my hands. I'm afraid they're not quite

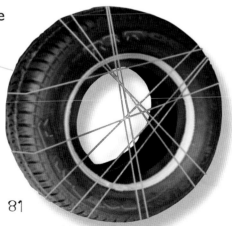

fit for fishing. But don't you worry, Angel-fish, you're still going fishing. Your big brothers, Mark and Derek, are taking you. Isn't that great?"

I just stare at my dad, too shocked to speak. I guess he thinks that means yes, on account of the next thing he does is pat me on the head with his swollen hand and tells me he's glad I'm not disappointed.

NOT DISAPPOINTED? To have to go fishing with my duelling dumb-bell brothers and not Dad? Not disappointed that I won't be able to try the Whirl-a-Reel?

Oh well, I do my best to try and smile so Dad doesn't feel bad.

We pile into Mark's and Derek's car and I'm beginning to think that fishing with my brothers might not be so

horribly horrible after all, seeing as fishing with two morons is better than not fishing at all.

Once we pull up at the harbour, Mark and Derek order me

out of the car to buy supplies.

"If I'm getting the supplies, what are you two gonna do?" I ask.

"Arm wrestle ... duh," Mark says.

And if it's not bad enough that my butt-head brothers are ruining my day, up walks Nanette Manoir, who cuts in front of me at the bait shop.

"Well, well. Look what washed ashore. Going fishing I see, Angela Anaconda? I also plan to have a voyage at sea.

And I'd invite you to join me, but we don't allow riff-raff aboard my yacht, which is French for *expensive* boat."

"I was here first," I tell Nanette.

Nanette pays no attention and orders something called sushi, which she calls a gourmet lunch, but I call raw fish that people eat raw! It turns out that the bait shop is also a sushi restaurant on account of they sell the good pieces of fish to people like Nanette to eat. Then they sell the fish insides and yucky parts to people like me for fishing.

"I was here first," I tell the lady who's working at the counter, "and I want some worms."

"Yes, yes," says Nanette, "but your worms can wait and my sushi cannot." Nanette grabs a container from the old lady. "Charge it to my account," she says, as she walks out like someone who thinks she is important but actually is not.

"Have fun on your yuck-yacht!" I call after Nanette not loud enough for her to hear me. "And don't worry about me, because pretty soon I'm going to be knee-deep in fish up to my knees. My own fish that I caught myself, which I even plan to cook myself, so it will be cooked and not RAW!"

## CHAPTER 4

Mark and Derek and I finally get everything, including ourselves, into the boat.

"Well," I ask. "What first?"

"ROW!" they tell me, as they each hand me an oar.

"The best fishing's at the centre of the lake," Derek explains, as he pops open a can of root beer. "So row!" Mark nods, taking the can from Derek.

"But how come I have to do all the rowing?" I ask.

"Duh," says Derek, "so *we* can do all the fishing."

"You didn't think you were actually going to fish, did you?" adds Mark.

So for the next two hours I row the boat, put bait on Mark's and Derek's hooks, and I even have to climb a tree to untangle Mark's fishing line. And to make bad matters worse, Nanette Manoir keeps skiing by in her fancy un-French boat, splashing water on me. She thinks she's so great just because she can put two sticks on her feet and be pulled around on top of the water.

And meanwhile, Mark and Derek haven't even caught one fish, on account of they're using fake plastic bait in the shape of glittery fish with feathers on them – like any real fish would ever be dumb enough to eat those!

Finally Mark and Derek decide that their fancy bait must be too good for the fish in this lake, and they tell me to break out the worms. Only now I can't find the container I got from the bait lady, on account of the boat is so full of Mark's and Derek's empty root beer cans.

"No worms, no fish," says Derek. "Angela, pass me a root beer. Fishing's over."

"OVER!" I exclaim. "After all this rowing and untangling and being splashed by Nanette Manoir,

you're just going to quit fishing when you haven't even caught a single fish?"

Mark and Derek look at each other and nod. "Yeah," they say, "totally. Now rest your arms. We need you to row back later."

And as Mark and Derek are laughing, and I am thinking that things can't get any worse, Nanette Manoir skis by one more time.

"Well, if it isn't Angela Angler-conda," she says. "What's the matter? I don't see any fish in your boat. I guess you've been too busy rowing to catch anything. Ever heard of something called a motor? My yacht has six of them!"

Then Alfredo revs up their motors and they drench me with a big wave of water.

"Ever hear of something called a brain?" I call after her, but she's already skied off to ruin someone else's day.

## Chapter 5

So now I am looking at the bright sun shining down on the glittery water and I am thinking to myself that the next time I go fishing, things will be very different. And a lot more fun. My bumbling brothers won't be bosses of the boat when I have things my way.

First of all, there will be a nasty lake monster on the loose.

"Look out!" I will warn my brothers, but it will be too late, because the nasty lake monster will flip the boat and send my brothers tumbling into the water.

"Never fear, my sunken siblings," I will tell them, "I'll save you!" Because, as Dad promised, I am the first to use the Whirl-a-Reel! Then I will charge in on a seahorse, twirling my Whirl-a-Reel like a lasso, cowboy-style.

Just as the lake monster is about to swallow my brothers,

*I will cast the Whirl–a-Reel and catch Mark and Derek by their feet, saving them from the jaws of the lake monster. But as I swing my brothers around my head, they will get caught up in seaweed and be wrapped up tight like sushi. Then I will serve my freshly-rolled brothers to Nannoying Manoir, who I'm sure will find them very tasty!*

*Next I will hook Nanette and the sticks on her feet to the back of my boat, and she will water-ski from behind it with my bite-sized, seaweed brothers. "Perhaps you'd enjoy some fast food ..." I will tell Nanette as I go faster and faster.*

*"Lucky for you, Ninnie Wart, this boat has a motor, which is French for 'you're going into a tree!'" Then I will make a very sharp turn and send Nanette smack into the tallest swamp tree, and my brothers will go flying through the air ... never to be heard from again.*

It makes me laugh just thinking about it. But then I remember that I am not in charge of the boat today and my brothers have not flown through the air, never to be heard from again.

Well, I think to myself, I think it's time for them to hear that enough is enough on account I have had enough.

"I'm sick of you two being bosses of the boat," I tell them. "You're going to listen to me for a change. I came here to fish, not to row or open root beers. So move over, my Neanderthal brothers, on account of I, Angela, your sister, have got some fish to catch!"

And my brothers don't say a word, on account of they are both sleeping. *Sleeping?* Thinking that I finally worked up the nerve to yell at them and they slept through the whole thing makes me so mad that I kick their mountain of root beer cans. *WHAM!*

The root beer cans roll all over the boat, and then I see something. There it is, peeking out from under a couple of candy bar wrappers – the white container from the bait shop!

"The bait," I say, as I quickly sneak the rod out of Mark's hand and dip the hook in the bait container. I cast out and before you can say "Angela Anaconda is the best fisherman in the world," I hook a fish! Not just any fish, a giant fish. I need all my strength to reel it in and haul it into the boat.

I guess all my reeling and pulling and fish-catching must

have been pretty noisy, because Mark and Derek, who can sleep through a volcano erupting, wake up just as I hold up my trophy fish.

"Hey, check out that fish!" says Mark.

"Whoa," adds Derek, grabbing the fish from me, "I must have caught it while I was sleeping!"

Then Mark butts in and says, "No way, dude! I caught it while *I* was sleeping!"

"Angela caught it while you were both sleeping!" says a familiar voice. I look to the shore and see Dad, waving his bandaged hands that aren't bandaged any more!

"Is there room for one more?" he asks. Dad explains that he iced his hands all day and the swelling has gone down enough for him to hold a rod. "But I don't think I'd be much good at rowing."

I smile and tell Dad that I can handle the rowing part on account of

I've had lots of practice at it. And I row back to shore faster than I've ever rowed anywhere before!

Dad gets on the boat and admires the fish I caught. Derek stares at it, pouting.

"I don't understand how you caught a fish without any bait," says Derek.

"I don't understand how you caught a fish at all," adds Mark.

"It was easy," I tell them, holding up the container I found, "on account of I actually found the bait."

Dad takes the container from me. He opens the lid, and sniffs inside. Then he does something that shocks all of us. He actually takes out a piece of the bait I used and EATS IT!

"Dad! What are you doing? You can't eat that!" I cry.

"Actually I can, Angel-fish. It seems that the bait that you found is high-quality fresh sushi."

"But, if that's sushi, what happened to the worms I bought?" I ask, totally confused.

Just then, Nanette Manoir's motorboat motors past us. "Pass the sushi, Alfredo," we hear her say. "It's time for lunch."

And you can imagine what happens next. Nanette lets out a scream to beat all screams:

"WOOOORRRRRMMMMSSSS!"

Dad smiles and holds up my huge fish. "Do you think we should share some of our lunch with her?"

And we both laugh so hard that we almost sink the boat.

# THE END

"Hi, if you've enjoyed this book, why not read some more books about me, Angela Anaconda, and the other folks at Tapwater Springs. We have a cool selection."

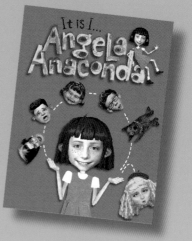

Coming Soon . . .

GORDY RHINEHART'S RAINY DAY
ACTIVITY BOOK

SCHOOL IS A NECESSARY EVIL

PIZZA WARS

FLOUR POWER